Arthur A. Levine Books

An Imprint of Scholastic Press

New York

BEAUTIFUL

The Legend of the Nun's Kung Fu

WARRIOR

by Emily Arnold McCully

Book design by David Saylor

The book is set in 13-point Monotype Fairfield Medium.

The art for this book was created using watercolor, tempera, and pastel on 140 pound
Arches Cold Press paper photographed against a background of Chinese silk.

LIBRARY OF CONGRESS CATALOGING-IN-PUBLICATION DATA

McCully, Emily Arnold.

Beautiful warrior: the legend of the nun's kung fu / written and illustrated by
Emily Arnold McCully.   p.   cm.

Summary: Tells the story of two unlikely kung fu masters and how their skill in
martial arts saves them both.

ISBN 0-590-37487-7

[1. Kung Fu—Fiction. 2. Sex role—Fiction. 3. China—Fiction.]
I. Title.

PZ7.M478415Be   1998

[Fic]—DC21   97-3823

10 9 8 7 6 5 4 3 2 1   8 9/9 0/0 01 02 03

Printed in Singapore   46

First edition, March 1998

Acknowledgments

Many thanks to writer and martial artist Barbara Nevins-Taylor, who first mentioned Wu Mei to me and explained her significance.

Master Ken Lo, heir to the Wu Mei Kung Fu tradition, generously allowed me to watch classes and shared his knowledge of Chinese history, culture, and martial arts.

Master Laurence Tan also graciously took time to instruct me in Shaolin history and technique. He showed me a video made at Shaolin Temple. Both men devote themselves to understanding and preserving endangered Chinese traditions.

Professor Lionel Jensen, Director of the Program in Chinese Studies at The University of Colorado at Denver, kindly provided a bibliography, encouragement, and expert advice. This book is dedicated to his daughters, Elena and Hannah.

Jonathan D. Spence's *The Search for Modern China* and *The Death of Woman Wang* paint vivid pictures of life in late Ming and early Chi'ing (Manchu) China.

Pronunciation Guide

Wu Mei: *woo may*

Wing Chun: *wing chuhn*

qi: *chee*

Shaolin: *shaow-leen*

Mingyi: *ming-yee*

Jingyong: *jing-yahng*

Long ago, in the reign of the last Ming Emperor, a baby girl was born in the Forbidden City. Following Chinese custom, her parents watched for signs of her true nature before they chose a name. Something in the steady gaze of her brown eyes struck deep in her father's heart.

"We will call her Jingyong, 'Quiet Courage,'" he announced. The infant seemed, to him, marked to follow an exceptional path in life, and would need the tools to find it. Girls born at court were sent to the ladies-in-waiting to learn their precious ways, have their feet bound, and pursue idle pastimes — never leaving the palace walls. "I refuse to do that to Jingyong!" her father declared.

Instead, he sent her to the tutors as if she were a son. She studied the five pillars of learning: art, literature, music, medicine, and martial arts. Jingyong was a prodigy, excelling especially at martial arts. Kung fu taught her to use her qi, or vital energy. With qi, softness could prevail over hardness, a yielding force master a brute one.

In kung fu contests Jingyong proved that a slight girl could defeat a brawny youth.

"Who will want to marry an educated woman?" Jingyong's mother wailed. "And one adept at kung fu, too!"

"She will find her own path," her father said.

One day, when Jingyong was riding in the western hills, Manchu warriors swept down from over the northern border and conquered the Forbidden City. The Ming Dynasty was ended. China's new rulers had separated her from her parents and ended the life Jingyong had known. From now on, she would have to make her own way.

Afraid and grieving, she took deep breaths to allow her qi to flow freely through her body. This helped her to concentrate and she thought of the Shaolin Monastery, where Buddhist monks had practiced kung fu for a thousand years. Jingyong set off on the path to Shaolin.

"I wish to continue my studies with you," Jingyong told the monks. "I practice kung fu as you do." She tried to keep her mind from filling with worry. Would the monks accept a girl?

"Let me show you!" she cried.

Finally, a monk stepped forward to challenge her. Jingyong defeated him. The monks were stunned. "Join us," the abbot said.

So Jingyong was given the name Wu Mei, meaning beautiful warrior.

She shaved her head and became a Buddhist nun. When Shaolin monks begged in the villages, they talked about the nun whose calm concentration never left her. Young men came to Shaolin to study with her and she taught them if they were sincere, and didn't just want to beat somebody up.

At the foot of Mount Song lay a village where the Wang family eked out a living selling bean curd. One day, the local magistrate ordered a cart load of bean cakes for a banquet and young Mingyi Wang delivered them. The magistrate paid her and she started for home, singing because she had never held such a fat purse!

Without warning, two men jumped out from behind a wall. One held a knife to her throat.

"Hand over the money!" he snarled.

Mingyi Wang clutched at the purse. She frantically looked for help, but there was only a tiny nun at the end of the street. Weeping, she held out her treasure.

Suddenly, a great wind sucked at them. The nun was drawing a breath! Her body seemed to swell until she towered over the thieves. Her hands sliced the air like knives. Her feet pounded the ground like thunder. The thieves went flying, head over heels. Then the nun seemed to shrink to her original size.

"Get yourself home," she said to the bean curd seller. "And be careful."

"Who are you?" Mingyi gasped.

"I am Wu Mei from Shaolin," said the nun, and hurried away.

So the Wangs saved the magistrate's money for Mingyi's dowry. Life was uneventful until the day a hairy brigand rode into town with his gang. He bought a bean curd cake from Mingyi.

"Pretty girl!" he shouted. "You'll make me a fine wife!"

"I will not!" said Mingyi.

"I am Soong Ling. Give me your daughter or my gang will break up your shop!" he said to Mingyi's father.

"Marry him!" her terrified father said. "Or he'll ruin us!"

Mingyi cried for hours. When she ran out of tears she suddenly remembered Wu Mei. The little nun could trounce Soong Ling so that he'd never bother her again!

Mingyi left a note for her parents telling them not to worry and went to Shaolin temple.

As she approached, the monastery bell pealed in the high thin air. In a courtyard, the nun sat like a stone under a tree. Mingyi blurted out her story.

Wu Mei raised her hand.

"Calm your mind," she said. "No problem can be solved by a drunken monkey."

Mingyi went on babbling.

"I've already solved it!" she insisted. "You just give Soong Ling a good drubbing!"

"I fight only to save lives," Wu Mei said.

Mingyi sank to the ground and howled, "*My life is wrecked if I have to marry that thug!*"

"You must save yourself," Wu Mei said.

Something about the innocence of this scatterbrained girl touched Wu Mei. Could the bean curd seller learn to be calm, to concentrate, and use her qi? Could she find her own way if she were given the tools? It would be a challenge to try to teach her!

"Do this," Wu Mei said, "tell Soong Ling that he must win you. Tell him you will marry him if he can best you at kung fu."

"What? But I don't know kung fu! Besides, he's huge! He would smash me like a bean curd cake!"

Wu Mei laughed, "It is not force that prevails, but inner strength. Kung fu takes a lifetime to learn. But this is an emergency. So I will give you a crash course. It will take a year. Postpone the wedding."

Mingyi was very disappointed. She had come all this way, so full of hope, only to be given a crazy plan. But what choice was there? She went home and told Soong Ling, who thought it was hilarious. So did all of his goons.

"Why not wait a year? How can I lose?" he crowed.

Mingyi left her parents and returned to the Shaolin Temple where the lessons began.

Wu Mei led her pupil to a pool of water.

"Make your mind perfectly calm, like this pool," she instructed. "Thoughts are ripples that only disturb it."

Mingyi leaned over the pool. Floating there was her own puzzled face.

The nun took her to a rushing stream.

Wu Mei said, "Water finds the path of least resistance. Nothing is softer than water. Yet it wears away the hardest rock."

"That's so," said Mingyi. "But what use is it to me?"

"Now look at the bamboo," Wu Mei went on. "When the wind blows, bamboo bends but doesn't break. When the wind changes, it snaps back like a whip."

Mingyi said, "Hadn't I better learn to fight?"

"You are learning now," said Wu Mei serenely.

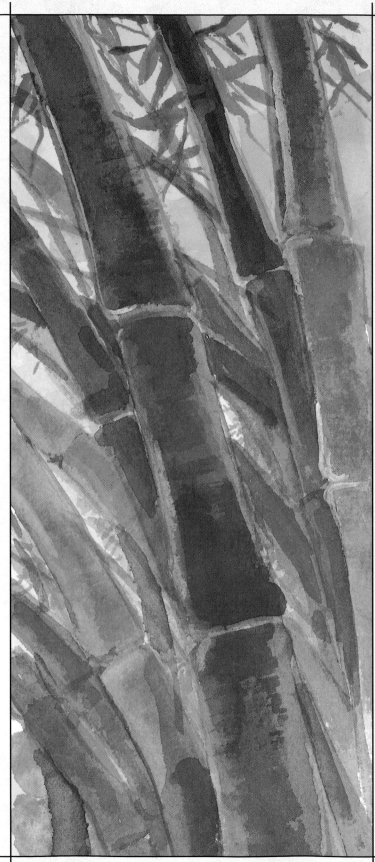

Wu Mei led Mingyi back to a clearing.

"Watch!" said Wu Mei. "The stately crane never loses its balance. It moves quickly and pecks at the snake. The snake coils and slithers out of reach, then wraps itself around the crane's legs. Each creature makes use of its body's natural strengths."

Wu Mei took Mingyi to another courtyard where five wooden posts were stuck in the earth.

"My plum poles teach balance and quick reflexes."

Mingyi climbed up onto the poles and tried to jump from one to another. It was impossible!

"If this is what I must do to fight Soong Ling, I give up now," she cried.

"Stay!" said Wu Mei.

Staying on the poles took so much concentration Mingyi forgot to complain. After a few weeks she was surefooted and able to wave back and forth. Mingyi knew that she was so nimble, Soong Ling would find it hard to land a blow!

When the nun asked, "What have you learned?" Mingyi answered, "To make my feet like roots and my body like a vine! Find the course of least resistance! Soft overcomes hard!"

"Now you must become perfectly calm. Concentrate on nothing," said Wu Mei. "This takes discipline. Meditation teaches it."

Wu Mei made Mingyi sit without moving a muscle. She wasn't even allowed to flick a fly off her nose. Whenever Mingyi twitched, Wu Mei rapped her lightly with a stick and Mingyi renewed her concentration on nothing.

Meanwhile, Soong Ling was dying of curiosity. He had heard that Mingyi was at the temple practicing with a woman! He had to see for himself.

He climbed up the wall and peered over. There was his bride-to-be, sitting like a turtle while a nun poked her with a stick. He went away again, chortling. Women were so foolish!

After a few hours, Wu Mei said, "Good. If you remain calm, you will know your opponent's intentions even before he does. Use his own force to defeat him."

As Mingyi meditated and practiced kung fu, she became ever more calm and sturdy. She began to feel that nothing could upset her. She had stopped being impatient and simply met the challenges of each day. The world outside Shaolin Temple no longer concerned her. She forgot all about having to defeat Soong Ling in order to win her freedom.

She was already free.

One morning, she greeted Wu Mei as usual, "Let's get to work, Master."

"No," said Wu Mei. "The time has come." Mingyi looked puzzled.

"The year is over."

"Oh!" Mingyi protested. "Am I ready, Master?"

"You are ready," said the nun. "It is up to you now."

Mingyi nodded.

"You have trained well. Your qi is good. You need not overpower him, only show that he has no power over you," said Wu Mei.

Together they returned to Mingyi's village. Celebration was in the air. Soong Ling and his band of ruffians swaggered about. A wedding feast with fireworks was already prepared and waiting.

"Concentrate. Flow like water, yield like bamboo," Wu Mei whispered, before slipping into the crowd.

The contestants faced off. Soong Ling let out a huge grunt. He lifted his fists and circled Mingyi.

"You are so tiny! I could crush you like a bean cake!"

Mingyi emptied her mind and concentrated. She could feel her qi flow freely. She could sense what Soong Ling was about to do.

He lunged for her, fists punching. She leapt nimbly out of reach and resumed her stance.

He attacked again, but Mingyi flowed like water. He swung his arm and she bent like bamboo. Then she snapped back, knocking Soong Ling off his feet.

Again and again the bully attacked, throwing all of his might at the little bean curd seller, but each time, she anticipated him. Finally, his own brute force exhausted him.

Mingyi gathered her qi with such powerful concentration that she lifted Soong Ling over her head and tossed him to the ground. Soong Ling's henchmen gasped.

"Wooooo!"

"Never mind," Soong Ling sputtered, struggling to his feet. "I'll find myself another wife!"

Mingyi's parents embraced her.

"Yours is superior kung fu, daughter," they said. "But now we have to find you another husband. It won't be easy!"

"I don't want to get married," said Mingyi. "I'm going to devote myself to kung fu."

She bowed to Wu Mei.

Wu Mei smiled. "Kung fu is the work of mastering the self and finding harmony with the universe," she reminded her pupil. "It is the effort of a lifetime."

"That is the way for me," said Mingyi.

And so it was.

Author's Note

The literal meaning of *kung fu* is "human effort." It denotes lifelong study, not only of combat techniques and exercise, but also of Chinese history, philosophy, science, and art. Recently, TV shows and movies have popularized the term kung fu in the West and made it synonymous with martial and performance arts. However, kung fu is primarily a means to physical and mental health and well-being through the development of a vital energy called "qi." It is first and foremost an effort of the mind, not requiring bravery or force.

One tradition establishes the beginnings of kung fu at the original Shaolin Monastery, where Bodhidharma, an Indian monk, preached chan (zen) Buddhism around the year 600. To keep the monks from nodding off during the long meditations, Bodhidharma developed a system of exercises, which later became useful in defending against bandit attacks. The monks of Shaolin became renowned martial artists.

When the Manchu overthrew the Ming dynasty, in 1644, Ming rebels often hid in temples, practicing kung fu for raids on the regime. Imperial orders were issued forbidding the common folk to practice it. Thus, the techniques were passed on from master to pupil in secret societies. In this way, Wu Mei's style has come down to us. Her plum poles can be seen at the present Shaolin Monastery, which has become a tourist attraction.

The more famous Wing Chun method was popularized by Bruce Lee and is taught by many masters. It is supposedly a style developed by Wu Mei's young pupil, here called Mingyi, who later took the name Wing Chun.

Whether or not Wu Mei and Wing Chun were actual historical figures remains an open question. In kung fu schools many different versions of their legends are told. All, however, reflect important principles of this martial art.